The Debt

CLINT WESTGARD

ALSO BY CLINT WESTGARD

The Devious Kind

The Adventures of Holly Amos

The Maleficio Chronicles

On The Far Horizon (a collection)

Nothing Was Delivered (Forthcoming)

Published by Lost Quarter Books
www.lostquarterbooks.com

This edition 2019

Cover image:
https://en.wikipedia.org/wiki/File:North_West_Mounted
_Police_1885.jpg

ISBN: 978-1-928035-49-7

From the personal diary of Inspector Archibald Constant Cumberland, June 7, 1886:

Fort McGregor, I am proud to record here, has been firmly established. I have already written my report to that effect and it is on its way to Superintendent Perry at Fort Macleod. We finished construction two days ago, and the men who were brought to help in the building have been sent on their way, along with my report. Only ten men now remain: myself, the eight constables, and the commissioned doctor, John Cabbot.

All of them are good men, in my judgment, an absolute necessity, for we are far from help out here on these lonely plains. Four of them fought alongside me in Riel Rebellion, so I know they are battle tested. Doctor Cabbot is newly commissioned, but he was trained at McGill and seems a competent man. He was raised in St. Paul, Minnesota, and tells me he spent some time in Deadwood and some other of the wilder environs of the American plains, so he understands well what our circumstances will be.

The other four constables are new recruits I chose

from the latest batch to arrive from Ontario. I had some time training with them in Fort Macleod, with Superintendent Perry granting me my choice of the new crop, and I am confident I have selected the finest among them.

Our purpose is to keep the peace between the Indians of this region, members of the Cree Nations, and the whiskey traders who have lately come into this territory, having been chased from the Cypress Hills and the Fort Macleod. After the troubles that have consumed the territories in these last years, culminating in Riel's second revolt, the Superintendent is taking no chances. The last Commissioner of the Mounted Police was replaced for his failures around the rebellion and the new Commissioner wants to see no such mistakes repeated. We are to be on guard for any such troubles that might arise.

The fort itself is located at the confluence of the South Saskatchewan and the Red Deer rivers, a largely desolate section of the Northwest Territories. It is, as yet, uninhabited, except for the aforementioned Indian nations and the whiskey traders. The nearest forts are Calgary to the west and Battleford to the east. There are a few settlements to the north and east, but to the west and south there is nothing but empty territory, inhabited by various tribes, as well as ranchers and others.

The Cree are to be confined to their reserves, as per the terms of the treaty they signed, but they have lately been ignoring those terms, the result of the failures of the agent assigned to them by the government. His name is Harold Groves, and he is a singularly useless man. The Indians do not trust him. I can only hope they will come to place their trust in my men and in me.

From the personal diary of Inspector Archibald Constant Cumberland, December 23, 1886:

I have been neglectful in my promise to keep a diary of

my command here at Fort McGregor. The lone entry on these pages has mocked me these many long months, yet it goes against my inclination to put pen to paper. I am no writer, and the reports I have to dispatch to my superiors, and the letters to my family are writing enough for me I suppose.

The winter, thus far, has proven to be harsh one, though the men's hearts are warmed by the approach of Christmas. Cabbot and I have done what we can, given our rather meager supplies, to prepare a feast for the men. There will, sadly, be little to drink, for we have nearly exhausted our supplies of rum and whiskey. What traders we were unsuccessful in chasing away, winter has succeeded in doing.

Even the Cree have abandoned the area for more pleasant climes, though where they might be in these territories, I do not know. Both rivers have been frozen since the middle of November and the temperature has been frigid for weeks on end. In addition to the cold, we have had so much snow that the drifts are nearly to the top of the fort's ramparts. It is a battle to keep the gates clear so that we can open them, and many men, against my orders, do not even bother with the gate when going out to scout or hunt for game. They simply climb over the ramparts and make their way down to the river valley where there are deer by the hundreds, fighting through the snow for food. They will have a fearsome struggle to survive the winter, if the snow and cold persist. In the meantime, we shall not lack for fresh meat.

A small note—which I hesitate to even put to ink, for that is more credibility than it deserves—several of the men have reported sighting a ghost from the ramparts, wandering out at the confluence of the two rivers. Cabbot says—and I agree with him—that this is likely just a trick of the wind, which can be fearsome here, and snow, preying upon the weaker minds of the group who tend toward the superstitious. I am inclined to agree.

From the personal diary of Inspector Archibald Constant Cumberland, June 21, 1887:

It is the evening of the summer solstice, the longest day of the year, and thunder rumbles in the distance. The summer evenings on these great plains are the greatest reward I have received for my career with the Northwest Mounted Police. When I stand upon the ramparts of this fort and stare off into the west at the long setting sun, the sky a marvel of red, purple and yellow, depending on the clouds that hover along the horizon, I have no doubts about my chosen profession.

Not that there is much reason for doubt these days. All is well one year into our stay at Fort McGregor. The whiskey traders have returned, but we are keeping a close eye upon them. Just yesterday I sent out two of my men to scout out their camps, where they are conducting their trading with the Cree nation. The Cree are at peace with us, and I believe I have gained their trust. Only yesterday the chief, a proud man called White Bear, said I was an honorable man.

Why am I so uneasy, then, as I put my pen to paper?

I do not want to admit it here, and yet, I feel I must. As I stood upon the rampart, gazing to the west, I saw a figure approaching along one of the old buffalo trails. The light was odd at that moment, for the sun was still bright upon the horizon, while overhead there were dark thunderheads. With the sharp glare of the sun in my eyes, and the shadows through which he walked, the stranger was more form than fact. By his general bearing and shape I first thought him an Indian, which was odd enough. Few of them travel alone, in my experience.

My immediate thought, given the direction he was heading, was to assume he was calling on the fort and that some sort of emergency was in the offing. I almost called to the other man on watch to put him on alert, but some innate caution stayed me. In the end that proved wise, for the figure kept a wide berth around the fort, heading toward the river. I walked along the rampart, following him as he passed alongside the fort and then into the valley.

As he came near the river, I felt the first spit of rain. There followed a flash of lightning and, an instant later, roiling thunder. Soon the fort was inundated with rain, followed quickly by hail, which sent me running for cover. As a result, I lost sight of figure as he entered the trees of the river valley and was unable to determine where he went.

Perhaps it was just the glare of the sun, or some other trick of shadow and light brought about by the evening and the thunderstorm, but I failed to get a clear look at him. What I could see was somewhat mystifying. It was as though he was an ill-defined sketch, by some lackadaisical painter, upon the landscape. He appeared to be wearing Indian dress, but it seemed, from my vantage, there was nothing to distinguish between the skins he wore and his bare flesh. His expression wasn't formed—he had none, nothing to distinguish him.

I read the words now and I acknowledge they lack all sense, but that was the impression I had upon witnessing him. He was something in the process of becoming, yet there he was, walking within hailing distance of the fort.

Most discomforting of all, when I asked the other man on duty that night what his thoughts were on the stranger who had passed by, he claimed not to have seen him.

"But he walked right along the northern edge of the fort and into the trees down there," I said gesturing to the confluence of the two rivers.

The constable shrugged helplessly, not wanting to call me a madman. "I'm sorry sir," he said. "I did not see anyone."

At the time, I told myself it was just a trick of the light and that I had let my imagination get the best of me. But I have not been able to forget the strange, solitary figure and his shambling walk. The more I think back on the incident, the more certain I am at what I saw. And the further I get from explaining it.

From the account of Daniel Archibald Cumberland, August 10, 1998

My name is Daniel Archibald Cumberland. It may be familiar to those of you who studied Canadian history some years ago. I graduated with a PhD, published a number of articles in leading journals and was hard at work on turning my dissertation into a book. I took a postdoc in Saskatoon and made sure to attend all the conferences and gatherings I could, hoping to secure an academic posting somewhere. It was then my life began to go astray.

My work focused on western Canadian history and was typical of the academy at the time. Those of you familiar with Canadian history departments and all their various touchstones will know where my work derived from. And it was derivative, of this I can assure you. Though many told me I was doing bold, cutting edge work, I now can see that this was far from the case. My work was no more remarkable than any hundred other students who worked in the history departments across the country. We all added something to the conversation in our narrow domains, but we only echoed what others had said about history in other places.

I was part of a chorus, while certain that I was singing lead. Yet I understood on some fundamental level that what I was doing was of no consequence to anyone. A pervading sense of dissatisfaction led me to be arrogant and dismissive of anyone I perceived as having anything halfway original to say. I would pick apart their arguments and find flaws in minutiae. How could they have managed the trick of saying something, when I had not, the unvoiced part of my consciousness would ask.

By and large I ignored these doubts and carried on with my work, desperate to be elevated into the academy. What I hoped to do there, I couldn't say. It was my goal, in and of itself. Life beyond that had no shape or hue.

All that changed when I went to do some research in a lost little corner of southeastern Alberta. Though my work was about the rural working class, I had spent little time among them. Still, I was convinced that I understood the overarching structures that shaped their minds, even as I dismissed those that constrained my own. I am embarrassed now to think of how great a fool I was, in so many ways.

Ostensibly my trip was to interview the editors of the, so-called, history books of the region. Each town had one and they generally consisted of a collection of life stories of all the families in the area. Most of the stories were written by one of the family members and detailed how they had come to the area and their lives there. They were utterly fascinating documents and I was excited to meet the people who had organized and edited, to explore their intentions.

It was during one of these interviews that I first heard of the lost Northwest Mounted Police fort. The fort had been established during the late eighteen hundreds, during the force's expansion throughout the Northwest Territories. It was intended to be a way station, on the way between Winnipeg and Calgary at the confluence of the

South Saskatchewan and Red Deer rivers. The Cypress Hills, the site of the massacre that had led to the formation of the Mounties, was to the south. But after barely two years it was abandoned under mysterious circumstances.

A kindly couple, Bill and Linda Cartwright, who had a ranch with some land near the confluence, told me about the lost fort. I half-listened to what they had to tell me, uninterested in some police post abandoned long before the settlement of the area, which was my period of study and reason for being there. It was the name which attracted my attention: Fort Cumberland. There had been a Cumberland, obviously, whose name had been bestowed upon the place, and I found myself wondering if we might be related in some way.

And so it began. From that tiny spark of curiosity bloomed a conflagration of obsession that consumed me entirely.

"We thought when we got your email that you must have been interested in the fort," Bill Cartwright told me that first day. "You'd be surprised how many people try to find it."

I admitted I found it surprising, for I could not imagine why anyone would have more than a passing interest in a fort that had been in existence for only two years, and that had been so long abandoned that no trace of it could be found.

"Well, it's no different than you," Linda said. "Why are you so interested in these history books? You have no connection to anyone in them, but here you are all the same."

She smiled kindly as she said, but Linda could have no idea the terrible effect her words would have on me. It was as though the veil of my miserable life had been pulled aside. I was not interested in these history books, these stories which I found repetitive and only mildly interesting. The lives of those who lived them were of no consequence to me, unless they slotted within the framework I

9

constructed of the past. These people didn't understand themselves and what they were doing, but I did, better than they ever could, or so I vainly believed.

But Linda's words made me realize the truth: I understood nothing of the past. It was utterly dead to me. All these people of whom I wrote in my papers weren't real, not to me. They were characters in a false drama I was constructing to prove a belabored argument. Once they had been living, breathing things, but they had never seemed so to me.

Worst of all, none of them interested me. Nothing else about my study did either. The endless books and articles on the subject that I would be forever striving to keep pace with, all seemed utterly dreary, to say nothing of my own writing on the matter. The future, the one which I had worked so hard to secure for myself, now horrified me. If I was somehow successful in finding an academic job, I would be miserable, I realized.

Yet I couldn't just abandon this work, now that I was so close to realizing my dream. It would be the height of foolishness. What to do? I kept on for awhile, interviewing others like Bill and Linda, and returned to Saskatoon to finish the article I was writing. It was painful, agonizing work and I hated every moment of it, despising myself for my cowardice at not abandoning it entirely.

The story of the lost fort—which according to Bill and Linda had been abandoned with little explanation—remained at the back of my mind all the while. At first I tried to dismiss it from my thoughts. There was little of historical consequence, it seemed to me, in an abandoned fort, where nothing of particular interest must have occurred, or else I would have come across it earlier in my studies. But the allure of it proved too much for me.

It was, I must admit, the fact of the fort's name that drew me to it. I felt a connection with this Cumberland, namesake of the place, as I did with nothing else I studied. It was possible that we might be related. My father had never mentioned having an ancestor who was with the NWMP, or who was important enough to have merited having a fort named after him, but he had no interest in the past, particularly his family's. The idea of studying the past, as I did, baffled him, and he looked at my profession with something like disdain. That is partly what drew me to my studies in the first place, and what kept me there beyond the point that they offered me any satisfaction. I wanted to prove to him that the world could be explained through the past, and that I could explain it.

Instead, I found that all meaning had gone from everything that I looked at, except this unknown man. Who was he?

From the personal diary of Inspector Archibald Constant Cumberland, October 10, 1887:

Harold Groves seems to have as his mission to undue all the good we have managed here at Fort McGregor. He is the most infuriating man I have ever dealt with and with his actions he has put the lives of my men in danger, as well as threatening the peace of the entire territory. He is the worst sort of scoundrel, as I have come to understand only too well.

It all began when I, and two of my constables, Terrence Cunningham and Neville Alabastair, made one of our last trips out to where the Cree tribe has been encamped for the summer. They will be leaving soon for their winter grounds. In fact, they would have left already had it not been for the blizzard that swept through four days ago. It left drifts of snow up to our hips, making travel impossible.

Before that, the weather had been mild and we had been enjoying an extended autumn. Not two days after the storm the weather warmed and the snow began its slow dissolution, at least for the moment. By the time the three of us set out for the encampment, there were only a few meager drifts of snow left, though all the low lying ground was filled with water and the ground was soft.

If not for the storm, I might never have known what Groves was up to. The Cree would have already left, and we would not have felt compelled to seek them out one last time to ensure that all was well. Instead, as we rode up to their encampment, we came across a second, just on its outskirts, where some traders had set up shop. There were two tents, along with wagons and some other sundries, around which were gathered a number of braves and a few squaws. All were visibly in a state of extreme intoxication, loudly carrying on.

I could not comprehend how such a state of affairs had been allowed to take place without my being aware of it. We regularly met with the leaders of the Cree and they had made no mention of it. I had been here a month earlier and seen no trace of this trading camp. When I turned to the constables with me they both denied any knowledge of the situation.

"We will get to the bottom of it," I declared. Turning to Cunningham, I said, "Ride on to the Cree camp and see if you can find White Bear. Tell him I would speak with him on this matter."

Cunningham nodded gravely and rode on past the trading camp, while Alabastair and I proceeded to its dark heart. There was no sign of any traders in amongst the Indians, but when I asked one of the braves—painstakingly using his own tongue—where they were, he pointed at the closer of the two tents.

The tent was dark, with only one lantern providing illumination, so it took a moment for my eyes to adjust. When they did they confirmed what was already evident to my ears. A man was carrying on loud congress with a squaw. Another sat with his arm around a naked woman watching this sorry display.

"What is the meaning of this?" I cried out.

The man atop the squaw raised his head and I saw it was Groves. He made no move to cease his exertions.

"What is the meaning of this?" the other man said, rising to his feet. "I've had no complaints about my wares from your men."

I turned to look at Alabastair, who would not meet my eyes. "Is that so? Well, I am their commanding officer and I will deal with them accordingly. Groves, how do you explain this utter dereliction of your duty?"

Groves simply laughed in my face, as though he could imagine no greater a fool than I. "What are you going to do Inspector?"

"Arrest you." I spoke the words before I had even thought them through and realized the entire gravity of what I had said. Groves went still at my threat, everyone in the tent looking to me to see what I would do next. I realized I would have to act, that having said the words in front of these Indians, the trader, and my own constable, I had left myself no avenue for retreat.

I turned to Alabastair, who still would not meet my gaze. "You will assist me," I ordered him.

Both of us went to seize the Indian agent who, realizing that I intended to act, had raised himself up off the squaw and was attempting to fix his pants up. The woman beneath him, I saw, was little more than a girl and I felt a righteous fury seize me. I grasped Groves by one arm, motioning for Alabastair to take his other, and we dragged the agent from the tent.

"I'll see you hang for this Cumberland," he yelled at me.

I ignored him, getting some rope from my horse and binding his arms. Groves fought against me until I struck him to the ground with my fist. I climbed up on my horse, Alabastair following my lead, and rode from the trader's camp, the Indians watching us all the while.

When I brought the scoundrel before Chief White Bear, and an astonished Constable Cunningham, he did not betray any surprise. I promised him I would see the trading tent dismantled and his people restored to him.

White Bear thanked me for my efforts, even as he appeared indifferent to them. When I returned to the trading camp, with Groves still in tow, intending to arrest the trader I was informed by the Indians who, to all appearances, had not stirred since I left, that he had ridden off as soon as I left the camp.

I left the tribe unsettled, even though Groves sits in our stockade awaiting justice and the trader has gone to the winds. If what the trader had said was true, then all my men have conspired against me, for the sole purpose of some stolen pleasure with the Cree women who had been seduced into harlotry. All the good that I thought I was doing here was apparently illusory. How could I have been so blind to the truth?

From the personal diary of Inspector Archibald Constant Cumberland, November 20, 1887:

After a month of waiting, word has at last come from Fort Macleod as to the fate of the man in the stockades. The news is bitter for me, as bitter as the cold that envelopes us. Harold Groves is to be released immediately and restored to his position as Indian agent for the Cree tribe. There will be no formal reprimand on my record, but it is made abundantly clear that I have overstepped my bounds.

The worst of it is that, with winter set in so heavily—again we are inundated with such snow I can scarcely believe it—Groves will have to remain here, at least for the time being. And likely for the entire winter, for I will not spare him the fort's only sledge. Already the men were grumbling because of the exposure of their sordid little scheme, though I have punished them lightly—at least by my measure. The complaints will only grow now that Groves is among them to foster dissent. It threatens to be a disaster.

Cabbot counsels me not to worry. "The men will

always complain about discipline, but, so long as you are not overly harsh, they will stand in line. They know that an uprising will only invite a harsher master."

I hope he is correct, but I fear he is not. The winters here are long with nothing to stimulate the minds of the men. It is so easy for malformed thoughts to fester. Last year, all one heard about was talk of the ghost amongst us. This year, will it be mutiny?

From the personal diary of Inspector Archibald Constant Cumberland, December 10, 1887:

We had a day without light, or nearly enough, with a storm so fierce that it blocked off the sun and left us in shadows. Cunningham has just been to see me. He swears he saw a man walking about on the ramparts as he left the cabin for the outhouse. There is no one on duty, of course, for nothing is stirring in a storm such as this. I told him as much, but he refused to believe me.

He insisted that we send men out to look, so certain was he, and eventually I was forced to relent. His surety disturbed me. It was as though he was possessed. The two of us roused two others, Cabbot and a new recruit named Messingham, and, bundling ourselves as tightly as we could, plunged into the gale.

It was a struggle even to walk across the inner sanctum of the fort to the ladder leading to the ramparts. The snow was heavy on the ground, up above my knees, and the wind was so strong all of us were bent over nearly double as we tried to make headway. The ladder was a sheet of ice; I nearly fell twice as I tried to climb it. Atop the ramparts it was impossible to see, the wind whipping the snow into our eyes.

Cabbot and I went one way along the wall, while Cunningham and Messingham went the other. It was so difficult to move, and our purchase upon the wall was so tenuous, that Cabbot and I clung to each other to keep our balance as we made our slow circuit. I could see nothing upon the wall, within the fort or without. There were shadows and shapes formed by the snow, but little else visible and the night was coming fast.

"There is nothing here," Cabbot shouted at me over the howling wind, echoing my own thoughts.

It was only when we arrived back where we had begun at the sentinel's post that we realized something had gone terribly wrong. We went around again, just to ensure that we had not somehow missed the two constables in the storm. There was no sign of either man anywhere.

We went below and roused the rest of the force, telling the men to go in pairs and to search every inch of the fort. The light was growing so poor by then that we took lanterns out to guide us. We searched the fort, even sending men up the wall again to see if somehow Cabbot and I had missed the two constables. After more than an hour's search we returned to our cabins to restore our warmth, having found no sign of anyone.

"What can have happened to them?" Cabbot said, shaking his head in wonder.

There was only one answer possible and we all knew it. "They must be outside the fort," I said. "They will not survive long out there. We shall have to go out again."

I could see fear in many of the eyes that met mine, a fear I felt myself, but all of us went out, even Groves, in search of the two missing men. We kept close to the fort, always keeping it and one other group of men in sight, so that no one got lost in the storm. Even then it was a miracle some of us did not become disoriented.

Eventually someone came across the two men. They had fallen from the wall through some mishap. Messingham was dead and Cunningham had a badly broken leg.

Cabbot set the limb and reported to me that Cunningham was still raving about the man he had seen on the wall. "He claims that it was this man who sent them both over the ramparts. They tried to fight him off, but he was incredibly strong."

I could only shake my head as I listened. Had Cunningham somehow gone mad? There had been no one on the wall. It was impossible in that storm. One constable had likely slipped and fallen over, taking the other with him. It was a miracle that Cunningham had survived the fall.

I could tell by Cabbot's expression that he was troubled by something. "What else is there?" I said.

The doctor hesitated. "He said something else. The man looked like one of us. He was wearing our uniform. He was an officer."

Both of us looked at each other. It was impossible. It had to be impossible. How to explain it? And yet, like the howling wind through the cracks in the logs in our quarters, doubt found its way in.

From the account of Daniel Archibald Cumberland, August 10, 1998:

An answer lay in the archives of the Northwest Mounted Police, but it was one that only brought more questions.

The archives were in Calgary, but I was able to order microfiche copies of all the records there, and soon my days and evenings were consumed in searching for who Fort Cumberland had been named after. Yet I found no mention of a fort by that name. There was, however, a Fort McGregor, which, by the descriptions I found in the records, sat at the confluence of the South Saskatchewan and Red Deer rivers. It had to be the lost fort Bill and Linda told me about, despite the different names.

There was a Cumberland though. Archibald Constant Cumberland was an officer in the force, joining in 1881 and rising to the rank of inspector.. By all accounts his career was promising. Letters and reports from his superiors were full of praise for his work ethic, his judgment, and his fairness. He was, it seemed, the ideal Mountie, a rare thing in those days, as my study of the archives made clear. When he was promoted to inspector, he was given the task of establishing what became Fort McGregor.

I was unsure what to make of this when I first discovered it and decided that somehow Bill and Linda had confused the name of the fort with the name of its founder. When I phone them back to inquire about the name Linda was insistent. "No," she said. "All anyone's ever called it is Fort Cumberland. I remember my grandfather calling it that. He was one of the first settlers in this area."

According to their history book, her grandfather had settled there in 1911, a little over twenty years after the fort had been abandoned. Somehow, in twenty years time, the fort's name had been changed, at least in popular memory, and it was now called after the man who had been sent to found it.

I could find no explanation anywhere for that. The history of the fort itself was startling brief. Only two years. Most of the reports that the inspector sent in the first year were brief and unremarkable. Whiskey traders were in the region harassing the indigenous and Mounted Police interceded in these exchanges. In the second year the reports dwindled – the winter was particularly brutal and the men were snowed in, unable to send out reports, which I gleaned from the reports of Cumberland's superiors.

The final report from the fort was not from Cumberland however. Over the winter he had been accused of murder and lost command. An Inspector McNevitt was sent to investigate the matter. He speaks of the men being in good spirits despite the hard circumstances of the winter and indicates that he finds the accusation that their commanding officer murdered one of their fellows to be credible.

He made no further report to indicate whether the investigation was complete and what happened to

Inspector Cumberland. All reports from the fort cease and the only one I can find is from one his superiors, reporting to Ottawa, to indicate that McNevitt has perished and that the men who served at the fort were being court-martialed for desertion, having evidently abandoned the fort. All the men were found guilty and discharged from the service, receiving no other punishment that I could find. The fort itself was abandoned, with no attempt made to resettle it that I could find, and no further mention of it made again the force's records. It was as though everyone involved agreed it was best left forgotten.

But the oddest thing by far was Cumberland's fate. He was not among the court-martialed, nor was he listed in the ranks of the NWMP in the years after. He had, it seemed, disappeared.

From the personal diary of Inspector Archibald Constant Cumberland, January 7, 1888:

So much has gone wrong these last weeks. I fear we may tear ourselves apart, and I am helpless to do anything to stop it. More than that, I am seen by many to be culpable.

We are twelve men with the death of Messingham, though he remains with us as well. We have still been unable to bury him. The ground is frozen solid as stone and the storms have been unceasing. As difficult as the winter was the year before, it has been harsher thus far this season. It has been cold beyond anything I could have imagined, the wind taking hold of my very bones, and the drifts of snow continue to grow.

Food is even becoming a concern, for it has been hard to find game and we have gone through our reserves much more quickly than anticipated. It is so difficult to move about with all the snow and the deer have been driven from this part of the valley by the lack of food. One man even reported seeing a pack of wolves—rarely seen this far east. They stalked him all the way back to the fort. Only the constant firing of his rifle kept them at bay. If he had been farther out, I fear what would have happened to him.

Cunningham recovers slowly, but he will recover, Cabbot assures me. There has been little talk of the incident since it happened, at least in my presence. But I have been told by Cabbot and others that Groves is fulminating against me, claiming that Cunningham and I conspired to remove Messingham. It is well known the recruit did not look favorably upon me and that Cunningham, along with Cabbot and one or two others, are all who remain loyal to me.

If it were not for the winter, I fear I might have a mutiny on my hands. If this terrible weather persists I may still.

From the personal diary of Inspector Archibald Constant Cumberland, January 16, 1888:

A number of us have now seen the being that Cunningham claims attacked he and Messingham in December. Alabastair was the first to come to me and confide, in private, that he had seen a figure, alone upon the ramparts, during another blizzard. He seemed reluctant to share anything with me, knowing that I was well aware he had been one of Groves' lieutenants.

"It was first thing in the morning, so the light was tricky, and I couldn't be certain of what I saw," he told me. "There was someone on the wall, looking down at me. He definitely seemed to be wearing our uniform, or at least something like it. I can't say what, but it didn't quite look right. The colors were a bit wrong, I guess. It was just off."

"How do you know it wasn't one of the other men?" I asked him.

He swore it could not have been. "That was what I told myself at first. Although it seemed strange that someone would be up on the walls at that hour, especially with the storm. And to be looking within the fort and not out. I can't explain it, but there was something eerie about it. So when I went back in I checked. Everyone else was in their quarters. All accounted for."

I heard a similar from another of our new recruits, a boy hardly more than sixteen. Duchene is his name. He came to the fort along with Messingham in the fall and has kept, more or less, to himself. To me, he appeared to be an impressionable lad, twisting this way and that in the wind, depending on which of the men took him under his arm to guide him. The feuding amongst our force seemed to frighten him, for which I can hardly blame him. It terrifies me as well.

A true disaster could unfold here before Superintendent Perry would have the opportunity to respond and deal with the men as he saw fit. Our growing hunger only makes things worse. That, and the rising fever from our close quarters and isolation, which is what I blame for these visions of the man upon the ramparts.

Cunningham and Messingham had simply caused their own fall, and Cunningham, wracked by guilt, sought some other culprit, even an imagined one, to blame. It was easy for me to dismiss Alabastair as weak-minded, for he had fallen under the sway of Groves so easily. And Duchene was little more than a boy. My own sighting of the strange figure walking toward the river, I long ago managed to dismiss from my thoughts, telling myself it had been some rogue Indian. There were any number of reasonable explanations for that sighting, I convinced myself, and anyway this new figure, now evidently dressed in our clothes, could not be the same thing.

This I firmly believed, until I saw the figure again for myself. It was during one of those days when it was so cold it felt as though my breath would freeze solid in my lungs. In the afternoon a wind began to howl, promising another storm that never materialized—the sky remained clear and pristine. The wind did stir up the most recent snow, powdery and light, to such an extent that it appeared to be snowing. Soon we could not see from the fort to the river.

I huddled over a brazier in the guardhouse atop the gate to the fort, alone on watch. Though it was a futile endeavor, especially in that weather, I insisted we continue our duty. Better to have the men active at something than to have us slip into torpor and bitterness. Men have gone mad in the winters in this territory from inactivity and I knew we needed to guard against it.

I must admit I was half dozing, unable to ward off my boredom or the chill, when I saw something pass by the guardhouse along the rampart from the corner of my eye. Assuming it was someone coming to relieve me, I hailed the man, glad to be able to return to my warmer quarters and my books. There was no response and no one appeared in the doorway. I would have dismissed what I thought I had seen as a trick of the wind, except that I had the strongest impression that someone was standing outside the guardhouse, just beyond the doorway.

It was a peculiar sensation, one that did not leave me, though I waited several minutes for whoever was out there to either appear, or for the feeling to pass. Instead, my certainty only grew and, with it, worry. I had no thought of it being the strange figure others had seen. Instead, I feared that it was Groves, or one of his men, lying in wait and preparing to do me harm. If a mutiny were to take place, they could not choose a better time to carry out their fiendish act while I was alone on watch.

The longer I remained staring at the empty doorway, and the swirling snow that lay beyond it, the more convinced I became that someone was out there waiting for me. If there was a mutiny afoot, I decided I would not stir from where I stood by the brazier. Let them come to me, I thought, even as I told myself that my impression was wrong. There was no one standing there. It was all a trick of the wind.

Finally, I could take it no longer. I had to know what, if anything, was out there. I pushed aside my trepidation and stepped out from the guardhouse into the teeth of the storm. It took a moment for my eyes to adjust to the gale, as I blinked away the sting of the snow. What I saw, I can still scarcely believe. I hesitate even to put pen to page, lest I awake and find it is all some terrible nightmare. But it was real. It was all too real.

The boy Duchene was crawling up the ladder to relieve me and was at the top rung, about to step out onto the wall, when I emerged from the guardhouse. I saw him first and registered the look of horror on his face. Only then did I notice the figure looming above him on the ladder. It was strange that I did not see him first. It was as though he had emerged from within the storm. He was wearing our uniform and, for a moment, I wondered who it was and why Duchene looked so terrified to see him.

Before I had time to think any further, the man had seized Duchene and thrown him from the wall to the ground below. I let out a shocked cry as I watched the boy disappear into the swirling snow. My voice must have carried, for the man turned round to face me. I took a step forward to confront him, wondering which of my men could have committed so heinous an act.

As I looked into the man's eyes, he seemed familiar to me, though I was certain it was no one who inhabited this fort. I thought of the others who had told me of the figure they had seen in the storm, and of the figure I had seen the previous summer. That half-formed thing that was not a man, but somehow appeared as one. This was the same being, I am certain.

We contemplated each other, I, wondering what sort of creature I was dealing with, and he, seeming to take a similar measure of me. I took a tentative step toward him, thinking that I had to do something—Duchene still lay below, and somebody needed to aid him. As I did so, he stepped back, vanishing into the wind and snow.

I pursued him to the far end of the wall, but could find no trace of him. Though I wanted to continue, to see if I could discover where he had gone—for he could not have simply disappeared, I felt certain—I had to abandon my search. Duchene lay below and I knew I had to see to him before he perished from the cold.

From the account of Daniel Archibald Cumberland, August 10, 1998:

I was consumed by the mystery of Archibald Constant Cumberland, abandoning my other research, my book, and my attempts to find an academic posting. For a time I pretended that I was going to write an article, perhaps even a book if my research showed it warranted, about how a fort named McGregor had become known in the popular imagination as Cumberland, the man who had established it only to vanish. There is something there, I would say to myself. But that pretense soon disappeared as well. It was Cumberland, and Cumberland alone, I was after. I needed to know what had become of him and if he had any connection to my family.

I don't know why I became so convinced we were related. There must have been dozens of Cumberlands, perhaps more, who settled in Canada over the last two centuries. It was a unique, but not uncommon name. The fact I shared another name with him seemed significant, but could just as easily have been a coincidence. Yet I was certain it wasn't.

By the end of my postdoc I had gathered what details I could find about the life of Archibald Cumberland, while my dissertation manuscript remained unrevised. Even though I should have been revising articles I had submitted to journals, or applying for jobs, or more postdoc funding, I spent my hours going over microfiches of Canadian cemetery records in the vain hope that I would stumble across an Archibald Cumberland.

In a sense, it was a search for my own ancestry. My mother's side of the family had a well-documented history, having arrived in Canada following the Napoleonic Wars. They were inveterate diarists, with many taking the time to record the family history, and making a point of staying in touch with even the most distant of cousins. My first encounter with the field of history had been to help my mother put together a slim volume on her ancestors, which she shared with the extended family at reunions.

The Cumberlands were different. They did not know where they had come from. They did not even know each other. My father had an older brother, ten years his senior, who he had neither seen nor spoken to in over thirty years. We had even been distant with my grandparents. I can recall only two occasions in my youth when I saw them. When they died my father attended the funeral, but neither I, nor my mother went.

With the end of my postdoc I found myself at loose ends, and without much in the way of money, so I returned home to Vancouver to spend some time with my parents while I sorted out what I would do next. My mother was delighted to see me, while my father, never very supportive of my pursuit of a PhD in History—"A useless degree in a useless profession," he informed me at one point—frequently wondered aloud at when I would be returning to work.

He was less than forthcoming on the subject of the Cumberland family history. "My brother might know about that," he told me. "I was never one to concern myself with those matters. I wanted no part of all that."

It was an odd way of phrasing it, I thought, to not want a part of one's own family and its past. The way he said it, gruff and dismissive, only convinced me further that I was correct in my surmise that I was Inspector Cumberland's descendant. To prove it, I found myself spending what little money I did have on a trip to Calgary to see an uncle who I had never spoken to.

To my surprise, he was quite interested in meeting me. "Your father never did approve of me. He took after my own father in that regard," he said, with a grin that suggested no small amount of bitterness.

His name was Richard and he looked remarkably like my father, with the same glistening eyes and long fading hairline. When I asked him if he knew anything about our family's relation to Archibald Cumberland, he told me, "Of course, he's our ancestor. I'm surprised your father didn't tell you. Where do you think the Archibald in your name comes from? It's custom in our family to name the firstborn son after him. My middle name is Archibald as well."

I was taken aback by what he said, which he noticed and smiled mischievously. "I have no children of my own, so you are the Archibald for your generation. Remind me, do you have any siblings?"

I shook my head. "No. I'm an only child."

"The last of the line then. And no children of your own yet, I'm guessing? People are waiting so much longer now for that."

I shook my head again, not wanting to discuss my romantic entanglements, such as they were, with a complete stranger.

"Well, it falls to you to carry on the line," he said, with a gravity that surprised me. "I always knew that Robert would want a conventional life, so I never particularly concerned myself with the matter. You will not be as lucky as I was."

"What does it matter whether or not I carry on the line?" I said, attempting to match his earlier grin, sharing in the ridiculousness of it all. "Are we sons of Anastasia or some other lost princeling?"

My uncle frowned and shook his head. "Your father really has told you nothing. I suppose he's tried to ignore it. He always refused to accept that it could be true. But he knows our family owes a debt. And it may come to you to pay it."

"What kind of debt?" I asked, more baffled than afraid. My fear would come later and far too late.

"You should ask Robert. He owes you an explanation. A father owes a son that much at least."

He would say no more on the matter and I returned home, mystified. When I tried to broach the subject with my father, mentioning that I had been to see his brother while researching some family history, he grew very quiet and forbade me from discussing the matter further. I would not be so easily dissuaded.

"He told me I should talk to you about why I am named Archibald. He said you owed me an explanation."

"Only one of us has a debt here," he said, going red with anger. "I'll not waste my time with old fables. If you want to continue to waste your time with this nonsense, you can start paying rent, or do it under someone else's roof."

I wanted to argue with him, to force him to tell me, but I knew it was no use. He would never budge on the matter. I left home the next day, with little money and no place to go, the only thought in my mind that I had to find my answers to these questions in some way.

From the personal diary of Inspector Archibald Constant Cumberland, February 10, 1888:

It has been nearly a month since I put pen to paper in this diary. So much has happened since then that I scarcely recognize my own thoughts here. They seem those of another person, tinged with madness. I would not believe it, if I had not experienced these events myself.

But I was witness to the events I described—more than a witness, I suppose—and now I am living with consequences of that terrible day.

The boy Duchene perished from his fall. Not immediately. When I found him on the ground he was still alive, though barely conscious and shivering terribly from the cold. I tried calling out for help, but no one could hear me over the gale, and so I had to go and rouse Cabbot and some others to bring him within the fort and see to his injuries. They were grievous. Cabbot noted he had broken several ribs, at least one of which had punctured his lung. Furthermore, his left leg had been shattered in several places, as well as his wrist. He was bleeding internally from these injuries, or perhaps others that we could not see, and he did not live out the night.

That night changed everything though, for as Duchene passed in and out of consciousness in his last hours, he raved wildly about his attack. He described a scene similar to the one I had witnessed. Only he had not seen two men upon the ramparts, one a stranger throwing him from the ladder and one me, emerging from the guardhouse in time to see it happen. He was certain, absolutely so, that the man who had pushed him from the ladder had been me.

Cabbot spoke with the boy, as I looked on in disbelief, asking him if he could not have been mistaken. Surely the wind and snow had obscured his attacker's face.

But Duchene denied it. "His face was near enough to mine, I could feel his breath. It could be no one else."

His certainty led me to doubt my own version of events. What had I seen in the snow? What had I done?

Word spread through the ranks quickly—there could be no secrets in a fort of eleven inhabitants. After Duchene died, Groves and several of his supporters demanded an investigation of the incident. They could smell blood. I did little to help my own defense, I must admit. I was distraught from what had happened to Duchene and had lost all sense of reason due to what I had witnessed and what he had accused me of. My rantings about the figure I had seen in the snow, who had pushed Duchene to his death, seemed either too self-interested by half, or the ravings of a lunatic.

Even Cabbot had his doubts, I could tell. He assured me he believed my story, as I begged him to, but his expression was filled with sorrow at what I had become. It was little surprise that I was soon thrown into our lonely cell, pending a trial. Groves and his men insisted upon it, and Cabbot, I am sure, felt compelled to comply with their demands, lest he be accused of aiding a murderer.

Here I have remained for over a month as Cabbot and Groves struggle for control of the fort. Cabbot has at least managed to postpone a trial for me until such time as an

Inspector can be sent from one of the other forts to investigate the matter. Given the winter we are having—the storms and the cold are unceasing—it may not be until spring that someone arrives.

No one has yet been sent to Fort Macleod to notify them of what has befallen us here. Cabbot refuses, declaring it unsafe to send any men on such a journey, while Groves accuses him of stalling for time. There is probably truth to both. In the meantime, we remain utterly isolated from the rest of the world, our food supplies tenuous, as is our sanity.

Mine most of all. The cell at the fort was not intended to hold someone for such a long period as I have been kept here. It has no stove or fire to keep me warm, though Cabbot insisted I be given a brazier to help fend off the bitter cold. For a time that was the only allowance given me, but Cabbot has at last endeavored to bring my diary and a few of my books so that I have something to occupy my hours.

As Groves no doubt feared, I have used the paper in my diary to another purpose, crafting a report as inspector of this fort, intending that Cabbot should provide it to a trusted man to carry to Superintendent Perry when the opportunity presents itself. I fear I may not survive to see that day, if the winter keeps on as it is. It is so cold and I am given so little food. I am forever shivering and begging for more fuel for the brazier. The men who guard me—all trusted lieutenants of Groves—do so only reluctantly.

Cabbot has just now been to see me. I have thanked him for the return of my diary, and I must admit there were tears in my eyes when I did it.

"You must keep your spirits," Cabbot said. "I have good news. Groves and I have agreed to send two men—Cunningham and Alabastair—to Fort Macleod as soon as the weather warms a little. In the meantime, it is important that you do not despair entirely."

It was good news indeed, and I gave my report to

Cabbot to entrust to Cunningham. I shall set my pen aside now and pray for some kinder weather so that I can be set free from this terrible imprisonment.

From the personal diary of Inspector Archibald Constant Cumberland, February 17, 1888:

I fear the winter shall never cease. The cold has seeped so deeply into my bones it has become a part of me. My resolve weakens with each passing hour. I almost believe that I am guilty of the crime I am accused of. Worse, I want to believe, I want it to be true, so that I might be hanged and spared any more days shivering in this cell.

The wind howls unceasingly through the night, my only companion. I can hear it whispering to me. I can almost make out the words it is speaking, which tells me that I have lost all sense of reason. Yet the words are there, all the same.

They do not bother putting a man on watch outside my cell during the nights, and even during some days. It is evident there is no point, for it is clear that I am utterly defeated in spirit. Even Cabbot has begun to visit less often, wanting, I am sure, to avoid being corrupted by my madness, in the eyes of those who are still loyal to him. I imagine those numbers dwindle day by day.

The last time he visited he told me that Groves had procured two Indian women. "From God knows where," in Cabbot's words. They now serve the men in every way imaginable. Cabbot looks both sorrowful and guilty as he tells me this. I can only shake my head in disgust and pity, while think longingly of their warm touch.

The last two nights the wind has been particularly bitter, finding every crevice between the wood, insinuating itself deep within me. I have not been able to sleep, in part because of the wind and cold, but mostly because the presence has returned. Just as I was certain in the guardhouse that someone was standing outside the door, now I know there is someone outside my cell. He has returned.

Two nights now he has been there. What is he waiting for? What unfinished business do we have?

From the personal diary of Inspector Archibald Constant Cumberland, February 23, 1888:

I have received visits the last two nights from the being. I do not know what else to call him. He cannot be human, though by all appearances he is. I now understand why Duchene was convinced it was me who pushed him off the ladder. There is more than a passing resemblance between us.

He still seems indistinct in form somehow, even as he presses his hands against the bars of my cell while looking down upon me. Perhaps it is the shadows, for the only light comes from the brazier that sits in the center of my cell, and its fire has dimmed by the time he comes. They do not leave me enough fuel to last the night.

He has just left me again as I begin to write these words, fighting to warm my hands enough so that I can manage these scratchings. Tonight he looked more like me than before, though I cannot explain exactly how. It is as though he is in the process of becoming me. A transmutation.

I know this will sound utterly mad. It is why I have told no one of his visits. He has said nothing to me, nor have I spoken, though I have been sorely tempted. He simply looms above me, watchful and reserved. I believe he is studying me. To what end I do not know.

I will try to sleep a little. It has been days since I have managed more than an hour or two, and my thoughts are foggy with its lack. I fear I will weep in despair at any moment. Most importantly, I must be prepared, for the being will certainly return. What will he do when he does? I must be prepared.

From the account of Daniel Archibald Cumberland, August 10, 1998:

I began my search for answers with my grandfather, hoping to connect him to Archibald Cumberland. If I could do that, then I might be able to determine what had happened to him following his apparent disappearance after the abandonment of the fort that now bore his name.

In theory, it should not have been a difficult search. My grandfather was born in 1919 in Port Arthur. It seemed unlikely, though still possible, that Archibald Cumberland was his father. Archibald would have been in his sixties, if not older, so it was more probable that he was my grandfather's grandfather.

I knew nothing about my grandfather, other than the place of his birth and the fact that he and my grandmother had spent most of their lives in Calgary, before retiring to Victoria. I remembered him as a sour-faced, silent man I had seen on the rare occasions my father had bothered to take us to visit him. My father, I now realized, was definitely his own father's son, both by demeanor and expression.

Toronto was to be the base for my research into my

family history. As an alumnus of York University, I could access their library and order the documents I would need, and I still had friends in the city from my graduate school days I could impose upon. I went from couch to couch over the next weeks as I ordered various government records, trying to trace my grandfather's lineage.

My great-grandfather's name was Desmond Reginald Cumberland, which suggested that he was not the eldest of his family, if my uncle Ronald was to be believed. Going from the Port Arthur records that I could find, both online and on order through microfiche, I was able to determine that he had come to the city in 1910 to work in construction and lived there for some years. But I could find no suggestion of where he had come from.

I was at a loss as to where to look next—I could not very well pour over the records of every town and city in Ontario to find out where he had been born and to who— until I recalled a story my grandfather had told my father on one of our few visits about a flood of the Red River in Winnipeg. Was that where the family had moved when they left Port Arthur, or was that where they had come from originally?

When I looked at the records in that city, I discovered that the answer to both questions was yes. My great-grandmother, it seemed, was something of a suffragette and wrote a women's column for a Winnipeg newspaper. This I discovered by happenstance while going through the files of the newspaper looking for birth notices for my great-grandfather, Winnipeg still being small enough in those days that the papers would record the birth of every child as notable.

I found the columns my great-grandmother wrote quite entertaining—I must admit to feeling a great deal of pride that one of my ancestors had so obviously been on the right side of history—as well as illuminating. In them she made reference to her husband, a native Winnipegger, according to her. There were some hints as well of a dark family history, though perhaps it was just my own need to find answers that created suggestions where none were.

Hers was not a happy ending, for in 1929 she walked into the Red River and was never seen again. I read her obituary in the paper and with it saw that she was survived by her husband Desmond Reginald and his brother Harold Archibald. Though it took me some time, I managed to find their birth notices. Both had been born after the fall of Fort McGregor and both had Archibald Cumberland listed as their father.

So it seemed that, assuming this was the same Cumberland, he had survived and escaped the notice of NWMP. How had he done so? And how was I to prove it?

In the course of my research I came across a fellow Fort Cumberland obsessive, a PhD candidate named Marcy. She was an American who had somehow become interested in Canadian history. "It was an excuse to get as far away as possible from my family," she told me. I wanted to ask her why that was, but it would have required sharing some details about my own family, which I was loathe to do, though I couldn't say exactly why.

I had met her at a conference some years earlier and when I ran into her again at the university library, we got to chatting about what we were up to over a coffee. She was heavily into writing her dissertation and I offered to read the chapters she had written, as one does. When she asked what I was doing, I told her I was looking into the history of the NWMP, implying that it was a project I was working on. A popular history, or perhaps a novel. I hadn't decided which it was best suited for yet.

At the mention of the NWMP, she became quite excited. "Have you ever heard of Fort Cumberland?" she asked.

"Yes, actually," I told her. "That was what started this all." And I told her about my visit to the Cartwrights.

"I'm sure you've researched it a little. Isn't it a fascinating story? The mad inspector people call him."

Here she was referring to my potential ancestor, Archibald Cumberland. "Do you know why they call it Fort Cumberland?"

"I was curious about that," I said. "In the documents I've read, they call it Fort McGregor. I can't find anyone who calls it Cumberland, and yet everyone today seems to know it as that."

"Fascinating, isn't it? It's one of the great mysteries of the fort. For McGregor is abandoned, without apparent explanation. Everyone is court-martialed, except for Archibald Cumberland, the man who founded it. He just disappears.

"So does the fort. No one can find any trace of it. Twenty years later when the area was settled, the fort was already gone. How? Maybe there was a flood, or the river shifted. But it's still strange. And by the time people start settling the area, everyone knows there was a fort there and they call it Fort Cumberland. And everyone has since. But how would they know to do that? People must have started calling it that after the fort was abandoned. But no one knows why."

"I've found Cumberland. At least I think I have," I said, telling her what I knew. "But I'm not sure how to connect the two."

We discussed various ways I could do so, most of which had already occurred to me. The Cumberland I had found would have died and been buried somewhere. There would be an obituary, or, at the very least, a death certificate. I would be able to find enough to prove that, in all likelihood, this Cumberland was the same Cumberland who had been with NWMP. Not definitively though, not without some other kind of paper trail to connect the two. And that was what I desperately wanted to do.

"You know," Marcy said, lowering her voice and leaning across the table, "My supervisor Joanne at UBC was obsessed with the fort. That's how I got interested in it. She would go out on her vacations—probably to the same ranch you went to—to look around and see if she could find where the fort originally stood. She even published a couple of articles in the paper about it in Vancouver. Sort of a popular history kind of thing.

"Anyway, Joanne told me that after she wrote one of these articles a guy came to see her, claiming to be a descendent of Cumberland. He had a document, which he wanted Joanne to date for him and sign a letter of authentication. Got pretty upset when Joanne said that wasn't the sort of thing a historian could do. Called it a useless profession."

I went very still at Marcy's words. "What was the document?"

"Supposedly it was Cumberland's last will and testament. But the guy wanted proof that it was that old. Probably just a scam."

"Probably," I said. But I knew that wasn't true. The man who had gone to see her supervisor was my father, I felt sure of it. And apparently, he possessed the last will and testament of Archibald Cumberland.

From the personal diary of Inspector Archibald Constant Cumberland, March 1, 1888:

The weather has broken at last, getting slowly warmer over the last three days. Cabbot tells me there is a Chinook arch in the sky, which means it will be even warmer to the west in Fort Macleod. He and Groves have agreed to send Cunningham and Alabastair to report to Superintendent Perry. In all likelihood, they have already left as I write this.

The possibility of salvation excites me. I must admit I wept before Cabbot as he told me the news. I was unable to restrain myself. For his part, Cabbot was reluctant to say much about the matter, beyond giving me the news. He would not meet my eyes, and when I asked him about the report I had provided him regarding my version of events, he avoided the subject.

His recalcitrance left me anguished. Events were transpiring beyond my control and without my knowledge. I felt then, and feel even more so now, that Cabbot has been withholding things from me. He may no longer be the loyal friend he was. If that is true, I have none remaining.

My fear that he has abandoned me was so great that I did what I swore I would not do. I told him about the being, who has been visiting me almost every night, staying for longer and longer, though still not speaking.

I could see the sadness in Cabbot's exhausted eyes. "What being is this Archibald?" he asked me.

"The one the men have seen. The one that I saw kill Duchene," I told him, speaking far too eagerly.

Cabbot pursed his lips and sighed. "I thought we had agreed that what those men saw was nothing but apparitions. It troubles me deeply that you seem to be suffering from those same delusions. I wonder about your state of mind."

It was a shock to hear from the man I had trusted like no other during our time here. I spoke with vehemence. "I have no doubt of what I saw that day, or what I have seen these last evenings. There is something here. Ask the men whether they think it has gone away. Ask Cunningham."

Cabbot shook his head. "I am sure Superintendent Perry will send someone to handle this matter expeditiously and fairly," he said. "You don't deserve to suffer as you have these last weeks."

He turned and left without another word, ignoring my repeated cries, asking if he was going to send my report along with Cunningham. I no longer cared if the whole fort knew of its existence. Superintendent Perry needs to know the danger we are faced with here. But Cabbot would not acknowledge me.

I now await nightfall and the return of the being.

From the personal diary of Inspector Archibald Constant Cumberland, March 26, 1888:

My spirit is broken. All is lost.

I struggle to write more than that, but I feel I must. This is the document that is proof that I have not completely lost my senses, though I am sure McNevitt will argue to the contrary. All my attempts to persuade have been turned back against me by him. He is a patient and exacting man, demanding precise explanations. All mine have been lacking in his eyes. I can understand well why Perry sent him. I often prided myself that I was as dispassionate an officer as he has demonstrated himself to be.

Inspector James McNevitt arrived five days ago, under orders from Superintendent Perry to investigate the affairs of this fort, specifically the accusation of murder against me. I can fault him in nothing that he has done since arriving. He has been more than fair, seeing to it that my quarters have been improved so I no longer suffer so greatly from the cold. And he has been thorough in interviewing me and, I must presume, everyone else here.

But he does not believe me. It is all beyond his comprehension. No matter what I tell him—that I have seen the being, that it has come to me night after night—it does not matter. He refuses to grant any credence to the notion. I cannot blame him, I would do the same in his position.

If he could see the being for himself he would be convinced I think, but I have not seen it since his arrival. As soon as the weather began to warm it began visiting less and less, like a memory slowing fading from my mind. I have begun to wonder if Cabbot is correct and I have somehow concocted the whole thing, the cold and my deprivation feeding my insanity.

But this diary is proof I have not. These are not the ravings of some lunatic. If I show it to McNevitt, he will have to at least consider that I am telling the truth. It cannot all have been my imagination. I did not kill that boy.

From the personal diary of Inspector Archibald Constant Cumberland, March 30, 1888:

It has all gone wrong. I gave the diary to McNevitt, as proof that I have witnessed this supernatural being, and that others reported similar experiences. I did so in the understanding that this was my last hope of demonstrating that my faculties are still driven by reason.

He has drawn a different conclusion, though. In returning it to me today, he said, "It appears your delusions have been a part of you far longer than I suspected. This is a hard and difficult place and it seems to have driven you beyond your capabilities. You had a greater responsibility to your men. And it appears to me that you have failed them."

"Ask them," I cried out, unable to restrain myself. "Ask Cunningham. Ask Alabastair. They will tell you what they saw. They have seen what I have seen."

McNevitt gave me the same pitying look that Cabbot had before and I knew that I was doomed. "I have. Messingham's death is being investigated, just as Duchene's is. Cunningham has recanted what he said earlier. He does not believe there was another person present during the storm. He and Messingham lost touch with each other and they each thought the other was a stranger. And they ended up sending each other over the wall in their struggle. A terrible tragedy, but an understandable one. I will recommend that he be given an honorable discharge from the service.

"I have sent him on to Fort Macleod, with word of my judgment for the Superintendent," he added.

He did not speak of my fate. He did not have to. I knew, as well as he, what he would be recommending to Superintendent Perry. My life is now at stake.

From the personal diary of Inspector Archibald Constant Cumberland, April 1, 1888:

A spring storm has spared me for the moment. After several weeks of warming weather and disappearing snow, where everyone began to imagine that spring was imminent, winter has returned with a vengeance. The temperature plunged yesterday just after noon and a blizzard soon followed on its heels. It still envelopes the fort, rattling its very foundations. McNevitt can go nowhere until it has passed.

The return of the storm has brought the being back as well. When he appeared outside my cell last night I shouted for all the fort to hear, that I was not a madman. That the being was here. No one responded to my cries, not even bothering to rise from their beds to silence me. Perhaps they could not hear me over the wind, or perhaps they believe me completely insane.

The being did not react at all to my yelling, studying me as he always does, his face expressionless. He looks more like me than ever, if it is possible. He could be my double, down to the gold band in his hat and his thin mustache.

When my cries roused no response, I turned on the interloper. "What do you want? Why have you been killing my men?"

He did not move, but I had the sense that he was considering my questions. Still, he offered no response.

"Damn you," I said, unable to stop myself from weeping. "I am to be hanged because of you. Do you understand? What wrong have I ever done to you?"

Finally he was moved to speak. He did so in a halting voice, emphasizing each word with care. I was so startled to hear him—and to hear my own voice coming from his mouth—that I did not know how to respond. "This is my place. It is not yours."

"What are you?" I said, my voice choked with fear.

"This," he said, extending his arms out.

"You are not me," I said to him. "You are not me. You are something from the pits of hell, damn you. You are damnation itself."

"I am this," the being said, gesturing to himself, and then pointed at me. "This as well."

As he spoke his intonation was less halting, his words more precise. It was as though he were getting used to his tongue. He repeated his gesture, pointing at himself and then at me. This time I understood his meaning.

"You are imprisoned here too," I said and he nodded.

"If I leave, someone must remain," he said.

It was, I understood, a proposal of sorts. "You wish me to free you and remain prisoner here."

The being nodded.

"And if I do not agree?" I asked, in a quivering voice.

He shrugged and held out his hands, a gesture I recognized well. It was my own. If I did not agree, my fate was in McNevitt's hands and he would take his offer to someone else in the fort.

"I will not simply agree to a life lived here in this fort," I said, in what I hoped was a defiant voice. "That is no life at all. If that is all you are offering, than I will put my fate in McNevitt's hands. He is a just man. You may be the devil himself."

He reached within his jacket and pulled out a piece of paper, handing it through the bars of the cell. I took it from him with trembling hands and read it over. The writing was in my own hand. How he had come by the paper and how he had learned to mimic my own scrawl, I could not begin to conceive. Yet it was no stranger than anything else that had occurred this night.

The document itself was brief. It stated that I would enter into a contract with this being, where I would remain in this fort until such time as he, or his firstborn, or his firstborn, on in perpetuity should return to take my place. In return for agreeing to this, the being would ensure that my life would be spared and I would be free of the charges against me.

How he would achieve such a feat was not elaborated on in the agreement. I suspected I knew how though.

"If you kill McNevitt, they will send another man to take his place. He will still hold me responsible. I will still be punished. You will not be able to leave." I handed him back his contract, but he refused to take it, smiling as he stepped back from the bars.

I felt horror overwhelm me. If the contract were discovered among my things it would be further proof—not that McNevitt required it—of my madness. A contract, in my own hand, with a being that, in his mind, did not exist would seal my fate assuredly. To this being, it did not matter. If I could not be plied, then he would simply find another in this fort who could be. So long as it stood, so long as we occupied it, people stood at risk.

And yet I did not want to condemn myself to pass the rest of my days in this place. Better to face the justice of man than live out interminable days here—eternity, if the contract was to be believed. For why should his descendants ever return once I had freed him? To say nothing of the fact that I would not live to see their eventual return. Even if I believe this being to be immortal—which I do not—I am, most certainly, not.

I went to the brazier, which still had some flame left in it, and, without breaking my gaze with him, set it to fire.

"Do what you will," I said, turning my back on him.

"I will," he said. By the time I turned around, he was gone.

From the account of Daniel Archibald Cumberland, August 10, 1998:

I returned home soon after to confront my father. He denied everything, of course, and refused to discuss the matter any further. I think he was tempted to throw me out of the house again, and, if not for my mother, would have done so.

So I went to Marcy's old supervisor, armed with a photo of my father and asked her if this was the man who had come to see her about Archibald Cumberland, claiming to have his will.

"Oh yes," she said without hesitation, upon seeing the picture. "I wouldn't forget him. He got quite angry when I said I couldn't do that sort of thing. Said it was important. That he had to know whether this document was actually real, or if he had been living a lie all these years."

"Living a lie?" I said, taken aback.

"That's what he said. No idea what he meant. I told him I could take a look at it and see if it looked like a will from that time period."

"And did it?"

Joanne gave a kind of shrug. "He would only let me look at the first page. It looked like a fairly standard document. It very well could have been from 1905. That was the date that was on it. But, you know, these things can be faked so easily. And there's a bit of a cottage industry around Cumberland. Collectors would be interested. They would likely pay a good price for something like that. If it was legitimate."

I thanked Joanne for her time and went back home, pondering to myself where my father would keep the document. Given his nature, I assumed he would have it secured in a safety deposit box in a bank. The house was empty that afternoon though, my mother out for lunch with her friends and my father at work. I went through all of his possessions, telling myself it was necessary, even as I knew I was betraying what little trust remained between us. There was no trace of anything even remotely of interest, let alone an old will. All it confirmed was my suspicion that my parents led completely uninteresting lives.

I became distracted by the search and, as I was returning boxes to one of my mother's closets, my father said, in a voice filled with rage, "What do you think you're doing?"

I was so startled I could not even manage a reply.

"We take you in and support you after the utter failure of your life and this is how you treat us? You owe us no small amount of money and you repay us by stealing more from us."

My father was shaking he was so angry. His accusation that I was stealing from them sparked my own ire. "I'm not stealing from you," I said, through clenched teeth. "You know what I want. I need to know. You owe me that much at least. You can't deny it any longer."

I had never seen my father defeated, but in the next moment I witnessed the visage of a broken man and it terrified me. "I refused to believe it for so long," he said. "I shunned my parents and my brother because I thought them madmen. But it was I who was mad to think I could defy this. To spare you what is owed."

He led me to the kitchen where we sat at the table and he poured us both a healthy dose of whiskey. Pulling out his wallet he fished out a well-creased piece of paper and unfolded it carefully. "This is a copy," he said. "I carry it with me always. The original is in a safety deposit box. If you want to see it, I'll take you there."

He handed it to me and I read what was there. The first page was as Joanne had indicated to me, a dry accounting of Archibald Constant Cumberland's possessions and who was to receive them. The second page read as follows:

"To my firstborn son, Harold Archibald, and to the firstborn of every generation that follows his, you are responsible for the debt I incurred at Fort McGregor. Know that I did it to save the lives of all the fine men there. I cannot expect you to understand, or to accept the heavy burden placed upon you, but know that the sacrifice is worthy. I hope and pray that the men, and their descendants, remember what we will do for them.

"As a mark of the debt I have incurred, and which will be passed on, I have given my son my name and charge that he, or his brothers, should he fail to sire a descendant, give the firstborn my name in perpetuity. That child shall be the holder of the debt upon his birth and shall carry it till the first of the next generation comes of age. The debt shall be repaid by one of you who follows me and for that I am sorry.

"The nature of the debt I have entrusted to Harold to pass on to his son. I will not set it down here, in the event that it falls into the hands of others. Some secrets should remain with our blood.

"There is one final part to this debt: Under no circumstances should any of my kin return to Fort McGregor. That place is barred to us forever."

My father knew no more about the debt Archibald

Cumberland spoke of in his will. "Dad and Richard didn't know anything about it, really. Just that there was a debt to be paid. I thought they were mad. And anyway, I wasn't a part of it. It wasn't my debt. I hadn't agreed to it. And Richard was the firstborn. But then he made his...choices, and you were born. You are the firstborn. The debt is yours now, until you have a child of your own."

"Do you believe any of this?" I said.

My father shrugged and shook his head. "I don't know. Father did. And I think Richard. At least, they thought it wise to act as though it were true. I'm sorry I didn't tell you. I didn't want you living your life according to someone else's design. The debt was all my father could think of. It drove his every decision. It ruined his relationship with Richard and with me. And for all we know, it was the raving of a madman. Or a fake."

Certainly, the image of Cumberland painted by the NWMP reports I had read was of a man losing his grip with reality. From that vantage point, the will was, in all likelihood, the ravings of a lunatic, as my father would have it. Yet I did not believe it was, even if I could not explain why I felt so certain.

It was the same surety that had led me to the discovery of Inspector Cumberland and the terrible hold he had over all his descendants. The debt, or the idea of it, had ruined everyone it had touched. It had torn apart my father's family and led my great-grandmother to lose herself in the current of the Red River—though I had no way of knowing this was the case, I felt it had to be so. Even in trying to escape it, my father had ended up in its service, forever disappointed in the choices that I made with the freedom he thought he had purchased for me with his defiance.

None of us were free of it. Without even knowing it, I too had been fighting against it, throwing aside my long dreamed of future in a mad quest for the past my father had denied me in a vain attempt to save me from it.

Something, which had affected so many lives so irrevocably, had to be real, I told myself. It could not just be a fantasy dreamed up by a madman.

But I still wanted to find out just what it was we truly owed. What had Archibald Cumberland done to secure the lives of his men at Fort McGregor? Who, or what, had he made his bargain with? And for what?

There was an inexplicable terror that arose in me whenever my mind turned over those questions. It was especially odd given I had no what the answers might be. I wondered if my father and all the other Cumberland's had felt the same, if it was an instinctual response that we somehow shared. All of this, my compulsion to seek out the truth about Archibald Cumberland, and my father's equal drive to separate himself from it entirely seemed to come from the same elemental place. An animal urge, inexplicable and beyond all reason.

There was only one place where I might find the answers to all these mysteries. It was the place I was forbidden by the will to return to. A place lost to time, all traces of it vanished. But I still intended to find it somehow.

From the personal diary of Inspector Archibald Constant Cumberland, April 2, 1888:

I write this under the watchful eye of my enemy Harold Groves. It is to him that I have entrusted my fate, and the fate of all those who remain here.

After the being left me last night I was unable to sleep. I described my encounter in these pages, in the hopes that it would bring me some clarity and peace, but my thoughts remained troubled. Morning came without any resolution, only an ever-deepening anguish.

What would the being do now that I had rejected his offer? Murder me and assume the guise of some other? Or begin the murder of everyone else in the hopes of persuading me to his bargain? I fear I shall never sleep again, no matter the result. All remains in doubt.

I passed a restless day, plotting various stratagems to thwart the being, all of them coming to nothing. So long as I remain in this cell, I am helpless to stop the being, unless I can convince some others of his existence. The men doubt. They need some proof, and there is nothing I can furnish for them.

It was only as the afternoon began to draw to a close that I realized what I would have to do. I cannot bear to record it here, for it is too grievous an act. When this night is over, I will be culpable in a man's death, I feel certain, and deserving of the punishment McNevitt has planned for me. Yet I see no other choice that remains. It must be done.

As daylight began to wane a strange storm approached from the west, one that I could feel, without seeing it. The air fairly crackled with electricity and soon there was thunder and flashes of lightning that were visible even within my cell. A spring thunderstorm was strange enough, but spring had hardly arrived—even with the warmer weather of the last few weeks—and the ground outside was still heavy with snow. A thunderstorm in these conditions seemed impossible.

I knew what the storm meant though. The being was coming. And so I began to put my plan in motion. I wailed loudly, raving like the lunatic everyone assumed I was. One of the men stuck his head in to see what the commotion was about and I begged him to find Cabbot, saying that I needed to speak with him immediately. That the storm meant the being was coming and he intended to do someone harm.

Cabbot came as the storm reached a calamitous frenzy outside, sleet and hail rattling off the roof of my cell.

"What do you want?" he said bitterly as he entered. He had become angry with me for my descent into madness, which he considered a betrayal. My failures had stained his reputation, leaving him with no future in the force.

"I don't know what remains of our friendship and the trust we had. I hope something," I said to him. "I have a favor to ask of you. The last one I shall ever ask. After this, if you wish to have nothing to do with me, I will not blame you."

"What is it?" Cabbot said. His voice was hard, but I thought I could detect some feeling behind his steely eyes.

"I want Groves to watch me this evening. As soon as possible. Tell him I have told you I plan to escape. Or that I plan to end my life before I have seen justice. Whatever you think will work. But he must be here to keep watch."

Cabbot eyed me suspiciously. "What do you intend to do to him?"

"Nothing. No harm will come to him, I swear to you. I would not ask you to be a party to a crime, believe me. I have too much respect for you," I said. I was practically begging him.

He relented at last. I do not know what he told Groves, but the fiend has come to watch over me. He watches me continually, with great suspicion, as I write this. But he is here and that is all that matters.

"What are you doing?" he has just asked me.

"I am writing my diary. I fear today will be my last opportunity to do so," I say.

"Why is that?" he says, his suspicions growing.

"I fear what this storm brings," I say. There have been a series of storms all through the evening, one after the other, each more unrelenting than the last.

Groves laughs. "This nonsense again. You think some demon is coming in on the storm. What kind of heathen are you?"

"The kind who has seen the devil himself," I say grimly. He is surprised by the force of my reply and falls silent. I stare ahead, past him, out into the growing darkness of the storm, and wait for what I know is to come.

From the account of Daniel Archibald Cumberland, August 10, 1998:

When I arrived at the Cartwright's ranchhouse, Bill and Linda did not seem surprised to see me. I told them I wanted to see if I could find the remnants of Fort Cumberland, that I had discovered that my ancestor had been the fort's founder. Bill offered to take me down to the confluence of the rivers so that I could look after I had lunch with them. "It's hungry work," he said, with something like a smile.

I ate with them, trying not to let the growing agitation I felt show. Now that I was here, so close to the place forbidden me in Archibald Cumberland's will, my former certainty had vanished and I was filled with doubts. How could events of a hundred or more years ago, whatever they might be, still hold sway over my life? It sounded ridiculous when put like that. I could imagine my father saying it to me in his gruff, dismissive tone. The ravings of a madman.

But he had kept a copy of the will in his wallet all these years as a constant reminder, so clearly even he thought there might be some truth to it. Whatever truth that was. And I had to know, whatever the cost might be. That need was as elemental as the fear, which overcame me whenever I thought of the warning in the will.

Lunch passed with some more idle chitchat, which was a welcome relief from the various emotions assailing me. After, Bill drove me down to the confluence of the two rivers. It was near the end of June, but he still warned me about getting too near the water as the rivers were high from recent rains. We approached from the west, having driven back that way to find a bridge across the Red Deer. On either side of us the two rivers snaked and curled, drawing nearer and nearer, creating a thin peninsula of land, verdant and green.

Bill took the truck across a texas gate and into a pasture, where we passed idling cattle, their calves frolicking at their sides. The sky above was vast, dwarfing all that stood on the prairies, with only a few scuttling clouds upon it. I could not picture a more idyllic scene, and yet I grew more and more terrified the closer we came to the confluence. The rivers on either side felt like the jaws of some great unknown beast that might snap close around me.

We came right to the edge of the river valley, looking down from the high ground at the confluence. It was not so large as I had imagined it being. There were two islands, running almost parallel in the middle of the new river, distorting its size somewhat. Bill gestured at them. "Some say that's where the real confluence is. Or was, back in the day. Somewhere around here, where we're standing, is where you'd build the fort today. But if the river moved, one of those islands might have been the high ground back then."

"Has anyone been over there to look?" I said, squinting at the glare of sun upon the water.

"Oh, sure. Lots of hunters go over there in the fall too. Plenty of deer. Even a few elk and moose. People have been across every inch of those islands and not seen a trace of an old fort. If you want my opinion, it's all along the Hudson Bay by now. Just got washed away when the rivers flooded."

Bill left me to my task, promising to return that evening. I watched him slowly disappear over the western horizon before I turned back to look upon the river, wondering how I should go about my search. Now that I was here, amidst the rivers and upon the vast prairie, the whole idea felt ridiculous. Where would I even begin?

I walked down to the river's edge at the center of the confluence for lack of anything else to do. The water rolled by steadily and I picked my way among the rocks that littered this side of the banks. I did not know what a fort foundation would look like, I realized, as I glanced around. I would not be able to distinguish between driftwood, a fallen tree, and the ancient structure of a fort, if any of it remained.

There was no point in my being here. I had come for nothing. Oddly, the thought made me feel much better, my fear and doubt vanishing, replaced by a certain clarity. Like everyone else in my family I had been in service to a piece of paper, the words of which had ceased to carry any meaning.

I was so lost in thought, contemplating my own folly, that I failed to see boat until it was almost across the river. Judging by the arc of its path across the current, it must have come from the first, and larger, of the two islands. The island where Bill had said he thought the fort had once stood. It was a canoe, old and unpainted, rowed by a solitary figure.

At first I was uncertain but, as the boat grew nearer, I saw that my initial impression was correct. There was no mistaking it. The man wore a bright red jacket that was immediately recognizable. As was the round pillbox hat on his head. I had seen that uniform in pictures in my schoolbooks. It was the uniform of the Northwest

Mounted Police.

From the personal diary of Inspector Archibald Constant Cumberland, April 3, 1888:

McNevitt is dead. It has all gone as I knew it would. I have told myself that the being orchestrated it all, but I was as much a conductor as he. I look at what I wrote yesterday and I wince at the lies I told myself. I knew what was going to happen and I played a part in it, because a life lived imprisoned in this place, with the chance for freedom, whenever it comes, is preferable to a noble death.

I have had enough of nobility and justice. It has cost me everything. I will face whatever justice awaits me when the time comes.

The being came during the storm and murdered McNevitt. Cabbot was with him and swore that I was the one who had choked the life from the inspector. Except it could not have been me, for Groves was outside my cell the entire night and I did not leave it. The fiend, who has ruined my life, provided my alibi and proved that I am not a madman and not guilty of the murder of Duchene.

Cabbot suspects that I am guilty of conspiring with the

being—how could he not, after I made him a party to the conspiracy? He no longer trusts me and fears what I have done. They all do. I can see it in their eyes. So be it.

He came to see me this morning, after all the madness from the night before had ceased, hardly able to meet my eyes. "You knew this would happen," he said to me. "That was why you wanted Groves to watch you. The one man who absolutely would not lie for you."

"Of course. What have I been telling you all this time? Only now will you believe it. The being has been to see me, as I have said, again and again. He looks like me. I do not know how it is possible, but he does." It was hard to keep the anger and righteousness from my voice. How undeserved it was.

"I did not believe you," Cabbot said, as much to himself as to me.

"No, you did not," I said, "And it has cost a man his life."

"It has cost more than that," Cabbot said, looking at me with fury in his eyes.

"What do you mean?" I said, my certainty vanishing.

"We found Alabastair and Cunningham outside the gate this morning. They must have been killed after they left. How no one saw it, or their bodies until this morning, I do not know." He paused, overcome by emotion. "What is this thing?"

I fell to floor of my cell and through my tears, I said, "He is the devil himself."

Cabbot knelt across from me and said in a tender voice, "What have you done Archibald?"

"I have given my life to him, in exchange for all yours. You must leave this place. All of you. Abandon it."

"You know we cannot do that," Cabbot said.

"You must," I insisted. "He will kill you all if you don't. He claims this place as his own."

"And what about you? What happens to you?" Cabbot said, straightening up. I could see doubt in his eyes.

"I stay here. My life is forfeit anyway. The Superintendent will not believe that some devil that looks just like me killed McNevitt, no matter what you or the others say. I have no life outside these walls to return to. You all do, so you must go. While you can."

I said the last with an urgency that frightened Cabbot. He left without another word, returning later that afternoon. "I have met with the rest of the men," he told me. "We have agreed to abandon our posts here and accept the consequences."

"They will be better consequences than those that you face if you remain here," I said, tears welling in my eyes. "Goodbye my friend. I wish you a good life."

Cabbot nodded, conflicting emotions moving across his face. "Would you like me to let you out?"

I shook my head. "Go. He will be along soon enough to see to me."

That was the last we spoke. No one else came to see me before they left. I spent the rest of the day listening to their hurried preparations and their speedy departure. The silence that came after was the most unbearable I have ever known. It was the sound of absolute solitude. I do not know how long it shall be until I am released from it.

I am free from one cell, though trapped in another larger one, as I write these words. The being has been to see me and we have signed the contracts, freshly written. My copy I have tucked into these pages and his goes with him. It is done and he is gone and I remain here, awaiting his, or another's, return.

From the account of Daniel Archibald Cumberland, August 10, 1998:

I stood rooted to the ground, watching the approaching vessel, feeling oddly like the terrified protagonist of a horror movie. Knowing I should flee from the approaching monster, yet unable to.

As he came to the shore, the man leapt expertly from the canoe and pulled it from the water. He looked like one of those costumed players at a historical site, except for his erect military bearing and the sense he exuded of a man capable of whatever the situation called for. It felt unreal, until I saw the haunted, ravaged look in his eyes.

"Archibald Cumberland," he said. I could not tell whether he was telling me his own name or asking if I was that person. Even he seemed unsure.

"My name is Daniel," I said. I could only hope I did not look as frightened as my weak voice sounded.

The man frowned. "The contract was clear. Only Archibald Cumberland, or his sons, can return here."

I hesitated, wondering how to explain this, or if it was necessary. This couldn't really be someone from that time, unaware of how many years had passed. "I am his descendent."

He nodded, as though he accepted what I said and gestured to the boat. "Shall we go to the fort? I have left the contract there. We'll both need to witness that all the terms have now been met."

My whole being told me not to go with him, that this was my doom. I felt as though my fear was choking me. But I wanted to see what this was. What had happened here. Some part of me still said that the will and the debt could not be real, that this was all some sham that would be revealed as such somehow. Either way, I had to know.

He started toward the canoe and I followed, clambering awkwardly into the front, as he shoved it into the water and climbed in and began to row. I sat facing him, studying him closely as he rowed, looking for signs that this was some kind of ruse. Perhaps Bill Cartwright did this to everyone who came looking for the fort. The idea was laughable, even as I fervently hoped it was true.

He was expressionless as he paddled and looked to be a man in his thirties, his face worn by sun and wind. Otherwise, he appeared to be the picture of health, tall and lean, his strength clear in the way he paddled. All but his eyes, which I was continually drawn to. They appeared to be the eyes of an old man, the light and spark faded from them. I shuddered to look into them.

Neither of us spoke on our journey across to the island. When we disembarked, the man—I still could not bring myself to think of him as Archibald Cumberland, for that would force me to contemplate the monstrous impossibility of his fate—led me through the thick cluster of trees that lined the bank to Fort McGregor. It still stood, untouched by time, and I was forced to come to terms with the reality of this place and this man.

He was Archibald Cumberland. He had lived outside of time in this fort, after its abandonment, for more than one hundred years. All without aging a day.

As that terrible realization settled upon me, a new question came to my mind that horrified me even more. If this man was Archibald Cumberland, as he claimed to be—and I now had no reason to doubt his claim—then who was the man who had come to Winnipeg and fathered Desmond, my grandfather, and Harold, passing on his debt to them? It now resided with me, and I knew, with an awful certainty, that I would be the one to pay it.

The fort itself was a desolate place, a simple stockade with only a few cabins for the men to quarter in. There was a rampart built around the wooden walls, with a tower above the gate that could be reached by ladders. The man closed and barred the gate after we entered, as I had visions of being gutted and left for dead, before leading me to one of the quarters built into the stockade. Once there, he reached into a valise and pulled out some worn papers and set them on the table, gesturing for me to look them over.

"It is all there, as we agreed to originally," he said, in a formal voice. "I think you will concur that all the terms have now been met."

I read the document over, my heart sinking. "I will not sign this," I said. "I am not Archibald Cumberland. I am not a party to this agreement. This all happened more than a century ago."

The man gave an odd shrug. "The signing does not matter. It is a formality. As you can see, the terms have been met. And I can go on my way."

I wanted to protest but I knew there was no use. It was all there and it was indisputable. The man did not linger, gathering his few belongings, and leaving the fort. I closed the gate after him and went up to stand on the rampart and watch him depart. He returned to the boat and paddled it across the river to the far shore. Once there he started marching to the west. I watched him for what seemed hours as the sun began its long descent, until he vanished into the horizon.

Even after all sight of him was gone, I did not stir from the ramparts and I was there when Bill Cartwright returned in his truck. I could see him get out and look for me, wandering up and down the river, searching in vain. The next day more people returned: other ranchers, police, search and rescue. There were boats and divers combing the river, looking for any trace of me. Searchers even came across to both islands, wandering through the brush.

I screamed and screamed until my throat was raw and only the sound I could emit was a croak. No one heard me. No one saw the fort, though they walked right by it a hundred times or more. It was as though I wasn't there at all.

I write this with shaking hands, in the hopes that it will be read, though in all likelihood it will be lost and forgotten, like everything else I have written. But it must not be. Somehow these words must find their way from these shadows to the light and be read. People must know what has happened to me.

I have read the contract again and again, and it is all plain to see. Archibald Cumberland made a deal to save the lives of all those at Fort McGregor. He agreed to the terms and now they have been met. And I shall never leave.

The following is an excerpt from the latest electrifying novel by Clint Westgard, available soon:

NOTHING WAS DELIVERED

Davis is a gun for hire, brought to Mexico City to do a job for La Familia, one of Mexico's most brutal and powerful cartels. All is not as it seems though. His handler, Aguilar, is also working for a member of Mexico's elite, a man of obscene power, who has his own plans for Davis.

Ines Suárez , a journalist with a source in the prosecutor's office, has caught a whiff of what might be the biggest story of her career, if it doesn't get her killed first. The federal police are about to move against the leaders of La Familia.

They are doing so under the orders of Gil Robledo, the prosecutor overseeing the case. He has cut a deal with a rival cartel that may not be as secret as he thinks, for a trap has been set and his vanity will lead him straight into it.

Connecting them all is Marina, a mysterious woman, driven to stop Davis from completing his job and setting in action a chain of events none of them will be able to control. But when Davis is hired to do a job, nothing and no one can stop him.

Here is a thrilling novel that will plunge you into labyrinths of intrigue, taking you from a violent underworld to one where wealth and privilege reign supreme, and showing the people who navigate the the treacherous streets that connect them.

1

"Café Americano y huevos rancheros," the waiter said, as he set the coffee and plate of eggs in front of Davis. "Algo mas?"

"No. Gracias," Davis said, the words sounding clumsy coming from his mouth.

"Para servirle," the waiter said, already walking away.

Davis watched him go a moment before turning to his breakfast, a soupy mess of red sauce and eggs sunnyside up atop a fried tortilla. While he ate he kept an eye on the two doors, which he had positioned himself to have a clear vantage of, one connecting to his hotel, the other looking out onto the streets. Both were more or less quiet, the morning still early, the Saturday night revelers he had heard as he drifted off to sleep still to emerge. He was not concerned about them. It was others, who, like him, were up at this hour with things to be done that he had to watch out for.

He finished off his eggs, leaving the dab of refried beans alone, and turned to his coffee, emptying half a packet of sugar into it. One of the waiters—the older one who hadn't served him—moved to the front of the restaurant near the street and began to remove all the tablecloths from the tables, folding them up and setting them aside. That done he began to stack the tables and chairs, moving them to the back corner of the restaurant.

Davis sipped at his coffee, watching this idly. When the man had finished each task, whether folding the tablecloths or moving a table, he clapped his hands together. Delight at a job done and done right. Without realizing he was doing so, Davis found himself nodding in agreement with each clap. He could respect a man who took pleasure in doing something well.

Davis was not his original name, his real name, if one believed in such things. He had left that behind long ago. There were times he felt regret at that choice, but only rarely. All choices had consequences. If he had not been willing to accept the consequence of that particular choice, the severing of all ties with his past, then he shouldn't have made it. Davis had been a name that came to him in the moment, simple and innocuous. It seemed to fit more every year, so common as to disappear as soon as it was spoken.

He did not linger once his coffee was done, wandering up the street to one of the pedestrian avenues that bisected the center of Mexico City, leading to the zocalo where the presidential palace and cathedral were located. He went in the opposite direction, toward the Palacio Bellas Artes, a spectacular neo-classical building of domed marble. He moved confidently through the scattered crowds, having passed along all these streets the day before, scouting things out, as well as playing the part of a tourist.

This morning he turned off the main pedestrian walkway to another, the 16 of September—Independence Day if he recalled the brief bit of Mexican history he had read—and went into a coffee shop. The Punto de Cielo, which he had also marked out earlier. Down the empty street he could hear department stores competing for absent customers with blaring techno. He ordered another café americano, not stumbling over the words, which gave him a keen sense of pleasure he would not have imagined possible, and went to sit on the store's threshold where he had a full view of the street and the passersby.

He drank his coffee slowly, apparently lingering over the early morning, though he could not resist a few glances at his phone to check the time. Timing was very important this morning. He could not be late for his meeting and he needed enough time to slip free of anyone who had latched onto him since his arrival yesterday. He thought it unlikely—there had been no signs he could discern of anyone following him—but one could never be too sure. Arrivals like his had a way of becoming known even in a place as vast as Mexico City.

Unlike the day before, when the streets had been teeming with people, a serpentine mass of humanity on the move, the streets on this early Sunday morning were quiet with only a few people out for an early morning stroll. Most of the stores had yet to open and even the ubiquitous police presence was largely absent. As Davis considered this, thinking about how it would make things more difficult for him to lose any pursuit—he had been assuming the crowds would be the same as yesterday, which was foolish now he saw—a woman stepped from the street into the coffee shop. She was dressed quite stylishly, an expensive white blouse belted over black tights, which suddenly, and to his considerable appreciation, women were now wearing as pants. She carried a large purse and wore very large sunglasses, masking her eyes.

She walked past him, a stern expression on her face, pausing for a moment, almost imperceptibly. It was impossible to say whether she had been looking at him as she went by. She had not turned her head. But something about the way in which she had slowed just as she came abreast of where he sat made him wonder. Something about the moment felt off to him and so he got up and drifted down the street before she had a chance to order and return.

He made his way to the nearest metro station, Juárez, and took it south out of the center of the city toward the suburbs. As he had mapped out the day before, he exited at the Viveros station, emerging to find himself on a hectic street, crowded with makeshift stalls with vendors selling food, newspapers and who knew what else. There was a large public park nearby, which he intended to cut across, for which the metro station was named, but there were no signs indicating where he needed to go and he was left momentarily confused as to which side of the street he needed to be on and which direction he needed to go.

Sweat broke out on his forehead as he fumbled for his phone to call up a map, while people brushed by him on either side. He was calling too much attention to himself here, though he told himself that wasn't a terrible thing. At the moment he looked like a confused tourist, not the person he actually was. Still, he cursed himself for not coming the day before to mark his path. He had assumed the park would be obvious from the street, but somehow it wasn't.

Eventually he found his way, entering the park, a veritable forest of trees, crosscut by broad pathways where he encountered joggers and couples and families. He affected to be a tourist out for a jaunt, stopping to look at various signs describing the species of trees being grown, or to sit on a bench and watch the crowd passing by. There was no one from the metro or the street where he had emerged that he recognized.

He took his time exiting the park, doubling back on himself several times, just to be certain. About a block further on he came to another small park with a yellow, ancient looking church at one end. There was a sandwich shop on the corner and Davis ordered one—a torta they called it—and returned to the small park to sit on one of the benches there and gaze at the church. The street was behind him, so he angled himself to have a clear view of anyone passing by on the sidewalk. He had no trouble spotting the old man as he ambled by, not giving any indication he saw or recognized Davis, heading east to the center of Coyoacán.

Davis finished his sandwich, taking his time and making certain as well that no one was tailing the old man, before following after him. He found him again in the square—really two squares linked at one corner—that lay at what had once been the heart of the old town, long since subsumed within Mexico City's vastness. There was a fountain at the center of one, with a statue of a coyote. Children played around, while people of all ages idled in the shade of the trees. The old man was seated at one of the benches on the pathway leading to the fountain. Davis wandered around the fountain, snapping a few pictures on his phone, before making his way over to the bench.

They both kept their eyes on the pathway and the rest of the park. Davis made a show of digging into the small backpack he wore to pull out a book, as though he intended to while away the afternoon. There was a group of teenagers sitting on the bench across the pathway and he found himself momentarily drawn to them—and distracted from the task at hand—their ease and laughter intoxicating. That had been him once, a lifetime ago.

"Are you enjoying your stay in Mexico?" the old man said in lightly accented English. He glanced fleetingly at Davis, but otherwise gave no indication he was interested in him.

"Yes. It's an amazing place. I feel like I could spend weeks here and not run out of things to see."

Davis glanced over at the old man, who was sitting with one leg crossed over the other and his arms propped on the back of the bench, looking for all the world like a retiree out enjoying a morning in the park. He was wearing a light grey sport jacket, despite the warmth of the day, over what looked like a golf shirt. He looked, to Davis' eyes, as though he should be wearing a hat to go with ensemble, but his head was bare with the silver hair remaining carefully combed back.

"Forgive my intrusion. I hope you don't mind. You have been to the Frida Kahlo museum? And the Trotsky museum? They lived here you know."

Davis did. This was where Trotsky had been assassinated. Ancient history by now, as distant a past as the pyramids north of the city, or so it seemed to him. "I'm going to see the Trotsky house this afternoon."

The old man nodded approvingly. "And of course you will have seen the pyramids?"

"I'm waiting till after the weekend. Less crowded I hope."

Again the old man nodded as though Davis' answer was the correct one, which it had been. "It will change your life. You're traveling alone?"

It was no idle inquiry, Davis knew. He nodded. "I prefer to travel alone."

"Ah yes," the old man said with a knowing grin. "You can't stay away from our beautiful women can you? Be careful. They will not be denied."

Davis briefly considered mentioning the woman from the coffee shop earlier, but decided against it. It was probably nothing and anyway he had lost her by now.

"How long are you here for?"

"I'm not sure," Davis said. "I was thinking of staying until Wednesday. And then pushing on to somewhere else."

"Ah, that's not enough time. But there never is, is there? Hopefully you can see all you hope to see."

"I'm sure I will," Davis said. "I was thinking of heading to some of the towns nearby as well. Is there any you would recommend?"

"Toluca," the old man said, with a firm nod. "Most travelers pass it by sadly. It's a small city, without perhaps the attractions that most travelers seek out. But it is not without its charm. I'm sure you will appreciate it."

"Thank you. I'll be sure to check it out," Davis said.

The old man nodded his approval and turned away, his attention back on the fountain. Davis looked over at the teenagers, wondering why he felt so wistful watching them. It was an unexpected emotion on a day when he needed to be focused entirely on the here and now. After a time he remembered the book in his hands and began to read it. He felt, rather than saw, the old man get to his feet and walk away. Ten minutes and several pages later he closed the book and glanced across at the teenagers. They had moved along as well, leaving the bench momentarily unoccupied.

He was in the middle of shoving his book into his backpack when he noticed, two benches down from where the teenagers had been sitting, the woman from the café this morning.

2

Fuck, was his first thought after he registered her presence. Panic surged through Davis before he clamped down on the feeling and mastered his expression. How long had she been there? Surely not until after the old man had left. But that only brought up the question of where she had been before, which was even more troubling. Again he had to fight back his panic, along with the urge to get up and leave the park immediately.

This could all just be a coincidence, he told himself, not believing it for a second. There was no such thing in his line of work.

He pretended to fiddle with the zipper on his bag while studying the woman from the corner of his eyes. She was intent on her phone, a glimmer of a smile touching her lips. For a moment he convinced himself that it was a different woman, similarly dressed. After all, he had only caught a glimpse of her as she walked past him this morning in the coffee shop. But the longer he studied her the more certain he became that this was the same person. Her sunglasses were the same. The purse was the same, as well. The blouse could be any blouse to his eyes, but it was white. And her face was the same, obscured as it was behind her sunglasses.

A beautiful face. Perhaps that was why he was so sure

he could remember it. You did not forget a face like that, framed by a cascade of luxurious dark hair. Not in the space of a morning.

The question, now that he had satisfied himself that this was indeed the same woman, was what she was doing here. Having managed to follow him this far without him realizing it, meant she was very good at what she did. It also meant that she could have left without him realizing it once his meeting with the old man was done. Or she could have remained out of his line of sight. That she hadn't told him she wanted him to notice her. But why?

Davis considered this for a time, making a show of reorganizing everything in his bag, while still watching her. She appeared to be paying him no attention, although it was hard to tell with her sunglasses. He decided there was only one way to know for certain what was happening and got up from the bench heading toward the fountain.

He made a circuit of the park, lingering here and there to take pictures. A woman was selling ice cream sandwiches from an old cooler and he bought one and ate it while picking over a stand of tourist trinkets. When the opportunity presented itself he surreptitiously glanced to the bench where the woman was and where she remained, not looking up from her phone. Though she could still be watching him, he noted, by the angle of her gaze.

Deciding there was nothing else to be done, he started north of the square, picking his way among the crowd on a busy street. He went two blocks before ducking into the first shop he came to with windows, a pharmacy. There he lingered by a display case, his eyes on the street to see if the woman passed by. Seconds ticked by and she did not appear.

As he pondered his next steps an extremely attractive woman in a vivid green skirt and red top approached him, her heels clicking loudly on the floor. He had noticed her standing in front of a small display table with a banner behind it when he first entered the store, along with the small line of customers queuing by the pharmacist counter, but he had given none of them a second thought, intent upon the woman who was following him.

"Buenas dias, señor," the woman said, with a broad inviting smile.

Davis gave her a distracted smile in return, not wanting to turn his attention from the street, but also compelled by the woman's beauty and friendliness to respond in kind.

"¿Está interesado en nuestro producto? Es muy útil para ciertas enfermedades." The woman's smile grew broader.

Before he could say no she handed him a sample box and he took it, noting her long fingers and manicured nails as red as her blouse. He wondered, while reminding himself he had to keep watching the street outside, if the woman was using the sample as an excuse to talk to him. That thought vanished as he focused on the box, which was for Canestan. He looked at the woman in confusion.

She could barely hold back her laughter now. "¿Está interesado señor?"

"No," he said. "Gracias."

Davis handed the box back to her, feeling his face flush a humiliating red. As the woman stifled more giggles, he decided that he had waited long enough and stormed back into the street. A quick glance around did not reveal his follower anywhere, though he was left with a nagging feeling he had missed her during his interaction with the woman in the pharmacy.

"Fucking amateur hour," he muttered under his breath.

Realizing he couldn't remain standing in the middle of the street or he would begin to attract unwanted attention, he started back the way he had come. After going a block, he turned right, proceeding in parallel to the road he had taken to reach the central square. He paused here and there to study something in the windows or pretending to consult his phone, but he did not spot the woman, or anyone else for that matter, taking an interest in him.

When he reached the street that ran south past the old yellow church near the park, he went down it, walking at a clipped pace and not casting a backward glance. As he turned to angle his way through the park in front of the church, he saw her, sitting on the same bench he had while waiting for the old man. She was following his progress and when he came to a halt at the sight of her, without even realizing it, she gestured for him to come over.

He hesitated a moment, knowing he shouldn't. But the whole situation—the whole morning really—had already gone sideways. She had seen him looking at her, had seen him stop, so there was no pretending that he hadn't noticed her. The old man would not be happy, Davis thought, as he made his way over. More importantly, neither would his bosses, the ones who had brought Davis here for this particular task because of his skills. They expected a professional, not this shitshow.

Davis stopped in front of the bench, looking down on the woman, a practiced indifference on his face, which she met with the same half-smile he had noted earlier. She seemed to be waiting for him to join her, but he decided to remain standing, hoping to unsettle her and assert some control over this situation. Though she didn't seem the sort to be fazed and he was attracting more attention again, his height and obvious foreignness drawing a few stares from passersby.

She gave no sign that she was bothered by his refusal to sit, leaning forward on the bench, putting her elbows on her knees and resting her head upon her hands, which she folded over and clasped together. Davis felt oddly exposed, like a specimen being studied, regretting not sitting, but feeling as though doing so now would be to announce a surrender. But of what? She was still in command of this situation, of that there could be no mistake.

"Join me," she said at last, somewhere between a command and a request. Her accent was American, though he could almost trace the fragments of the Mexican one that lay behind it.

He pursed his lips and nodded, sitting on far end of the bench, so that he was beyond her reach, but she was not beyond his. She swiveled to face him, leaning back so that her head rested in her hand, her elbow on the back of the bench, while the other arm was free. Despite himself he felt a stirring of desire and had to resist swearing under his breath again.

"Who are you?" he said, when she declined to speak.

"The important thing," she said, "is that I know who you are. And what you're here for."

"What's my name then?" Davis said, wondering if she would give the one he had traveled here on, or some other.

She laughed. "What are names? You can call me Marina, if it will make you more comfortable. What would you like me to call you?"

"I don't think we'll be getting to know each other well enough to be on a first name basis."

"Davis is it is, then."

He tried not to flinch and failed.

"Oh, I know all about you. And what you're here for. Like I said."

"You've made your point," Davis said, wondering how much she really knew about him. His name—that one anyway—was well enough known in certain circles. Given the skills she had demonstrated this morning, he had to assume she was ran with the same sort of people. That did not make her knowing it any less disconcerting. "What do you want?"

"Nothing," she said. "I'm only here to warn. You're being set up."

"What the hell are you talking about?"

"Your friend, Aguilar, he's not telling you everything. You shouldn't trust him. He's setting you up."

Davis eyed her skeptically. "And why should I trust you? You're just somebody who's been following me all morning. How do I know you're not lying to me?"

Marina stood up, staring down at him from behind her sunglasses. "You're a professional. You should know this job smells wrong. Something's been off since you got here. You should know that too."

"You're right. And the something that's off is you."

She shook her head. "No it isn't. Aguilar is setting you up. Don't you want to know why?"

Davis considered her question. "Let's say I do."

"Meet me tonight then. There's a place called Lucille's, just off Álvaro Obregón, north of Roma. Let's say nine."

She was walking away before he had a chance to reply. He watched her until she disappeared, heading in the direction of central Coyoacán. As soon as she was out of sight he rose and hurried back through the park to the metro station, trying to outpace his growing unease.

NOTHING WAS DELIVERED will be available December 2019.

ABOUT THE AUTHOR

Clint Westgard writes mystery, crime and western novels, as well as science fiction and fantasy. He has published *The Devious Kind*, a mystery, and *The Adventures of Holly Amos*, a western, both set in western Canada. He lives in Calgary, Alberta.

ALSO BY CLINT WESTGARD

The Devious Kind

A Mystery

The body of a local woman is found in a coulee on a ranch north of Loverna, her head blown off with a shotgun. New to town and the job, Constable Martin Thomas arrives on the scene as a spring snowstorm begins to wipe out all evidence before his investigation has even begun.

There is no shortage of suspects to consider. A spurned husband. A jealous lover. A betrayed business partner. And family members battling over an inheritance. All have motive and opportunity. And no one seems to be telling him everything.

As he tries to sift the truth from the lies, the snowstorm continues to build, leaving Loverna cut off from the outside world. And Thomas alone to face a killer who will do anything not to get caught.

ALSO BY CLINT WESTGARD

The Maleficio Chronicles

Luisa is always more than she appears. Rumor and mystery surround her. And strange events seem to follow wherever she goes.

Born in Lima, City of Kings, to a noble family, her father so fears her true nature that he banishes her to a convent. There she falls under the suspicion of the Inquisition and decides to flee.

Disguised as a man, she embarks upon a series of wild adventures, dueling, carousing, and gambling her way across colonial Peru. But everything changes when someone recognizes her for what she truly is, and soon she finds herself fighting for her very survival.

In a world where she will always stand apart, Luisa undergoes a strange journey, marked by betrayal and murder, terrible powers and mysterious strangers. *The Maleficio Chronicles* is her incredible confession and a story like no other.

ALSO BY CLINT WESTGARD

The Trials of the Minotaur

In the fifth year of the rule of Auten the One Eyed a
minotaur is born to one of Colosi's most important
families.

Taken from his mother as a newborn, exiled and cast from
his family, the minotaur vows to return to the imperial city
and take his rightful place as a patrician in the empire. But
the patriarch of the family, his grandfather, will stop at
nothing to see this blemish to his honor destroyed.

And so begins an epic journey, through lands beyond
imagining, marked by despair and exile, triumph and
betrayal. At its heart lies a quest to be free.

ALSO BY CLINT WESTGARD

On The Far Horizon
A Collection

Cattle rustlers on the run, caught between a storm and someone bent on revenge. A rancher finds a strange artifact in a pasture, that may or may not be of alien origin. A dive bar in the middle of nowhere hosts five criminals for a deal that goes terribly wrong.

These and other stories explore the lives of those who populate the west. Homesteaders with mysterious pasts they'd prefer to keep hidden. Women wronged by the men they love and caught up in events beyond their control. There are killers, thieves, cops on the make, and people just trying to get through their days with their eyes On The Far Horizon.

All of these characters, and many others, meet in this pulse-pounding collection that will keep you at edge of your seat.